The Wind Plays Tricks

Virginia Howard

illustrated by Charlene Chua

Albert Whitman & Company
Chicago, Illinois

The sun was setting over the farm when the wind rose.

It howled through the barnyard. It moaned through the meadow. It screamed across the pond.

The wind blew around and around and kept the animals from sleeping.

In their house, the Hens cried, "Cluck, cluck, cluck!"
The Little Chicks, always looking for excitement, shouted,
"Cheep, cheep, cheep!"

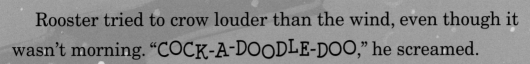

Rooster tried to crow louder than the wind, even though it wasn't morning. "COCK-A-DOODLE-DOO," he screamed.

The Hens clucked louder, the Little Chicks cheeped, and Rooster crowed. Their cries swirled with the wind.

Pig paced back and forth, safe in his pigsty.
"Oink!" he shouted at the howling wind. "Oink! OINK!"

Even though Cow and Horse were in the barn, they heard the wind. "M O O O O O!" Cow moaned. "M O O O O!" Horse bellowed, "NEIGH! NEIGH! NEIGH!" and stamped his feet.

But the wind didn't stop. It whipped over the meadow and whooshed across the pond where the Ducks huddled. "QUACK, QUACK, QUACK!" they called. "QUACK, QUACK!"

Turtle snuggled under an old log. He tucked his legs into his sturdy shell and pulled in his head. He knew the wind wouldn't last forever. Turtle closed his eyes and slept.

The next morning when the sun rose, the wind was gone—but so was Rooster! No one crowed to greet the day.

Pig peeked out of his sty, trotted to his favorite mud puddle, and plopped down. It felt so good!
Happily, he closed his eyes and said, "Cluck, cluck, cluck!"

One bright little eye shot open in surprise. "Cluck?"
He shook his head. "That's not right."

The Little Chicks ran around shouting, "Neigh! Neigh!"

"Moo, moo," Hen One called out to stop them. "No, that's wrong! Mooooo!"

Hen Two said, "Moo!" and then gasped. She stretched her neck and cried, "Mooooo!"

Soon the hen house was full of "MOO! MOO! MOO!" from the Hens and "Neigh, Neigh, Neigh!" from the Little Chicks.

In the meadow, Horse closed his eyes in the morning sun and crowed, "Cock-a-doodle-doo." He lowered his head and said softly, "Cock-a-doodle-doo."

"Cock-a-doodle-doo!" A smile spread across Horse's long face.

"Cock-a-doodle-doo," he snickered. "Oh, this is very funny! Cock-a-doodle-doo!" he chuckled.

Cow trotted up. "QUACK, QUACK, QUACK! Something awful has happened! Listen: QUACK!"

Horse tried not to giggle.

"I'll never be able to chew grass happily in the meadow again! QUACK, QUACK!" said Cow.

Suddenly, a voice came from the tall grass. "CHEEP!" it boomed.
Then, very softly, "Please help me."

And Rooster stepped out of the grass.

"My special crow has disappeared! Now all I can shout is CHEEP!
I'm so embarrassed! I've got to get my crow back before anyone
else hears me."

"I think I know what's happened to your crow," said Horse. "I have it. And," he said, looking at Cow, "I'm sure the Ducks are missing their quack."

"Quack," Cow agreed.

"Let's go find the Ducks," suggested Horse.

Turtle was on his sunning rock, watching the Ducks with surprise. They were calling, "OINK, OINK, OINK, OINK!"

"See? The Ducks are missing their quacks," said Horse.

"That wind played tricks on us. We have to get our sounds back!"

"How?" asked Cow. "My throat is filled with quacks."

Turtle opened his mouth and turned from Horse to Cow to Duck One. He snapped his jaws and bobbed his head up and down as the animals watched.

"I understand," Rooster said. "Turtle will hold one of our sounds at a time while we swap."

"That's a good plan, Turtle," said Horse. "We need to get the Hens, the Little Chicks, and Pig here."

"I can't go anywhere without my crow," said Rooster.
"Well, I have your crow," said Horse. "Let's swap sounds.
Rooster, give Turtle the Little Chicks' cheep to hold."

"Open wide, Turtle!" said Rooster. "CHEE-E..." and Rooster shouted into Turtle's open mouth. Turtle gasped, "E-E-EP!" as the sound went into his throat. "CHEEP, CHEEP!" Turtle exclaimed with delight.

"Rooster, you can take your crow from me now," said Horse. "COCK-A..."

"DOODLE-DOO!" finished Rooster, with one fast gulp.

"I'll get the Hens, the Little Chicks, and Pig," Rooster said, as he strutted away, crowing.

Soon Rooster was back, with Pig trotting quickly behind him, followed by the Hens herding the Little Chicks.

"CLUCK, CLUCK!" said Pig.

"MOO, MOO!" moaned the Hens.

"NEIGH, NEIGH, NEIGH!" complained the Little Chicks.

Horse folded his legs and got down on the grass, close to the Little Chicks.

They stood still. They had never seen Horse's head up so close. It looked like the size of the barn…almost.

"You have my neigh," Horse told them, "and Turtle has your cheep. We're all going to swap sounds."

"Cheep!" said Turtle.

"When I open my mouth," said Horse, "each of you must put a neigh into my mouth. Then go to Turtle, and he will give you your cheep back."

The Little Chicks nodded.

"After we all have our own sounds back," Horse told them, "I will give you a ride on my back."

"NEIGH!" said the Little Chicks with excitement.

They all did just what Horse told them, and then hopped onto Horse's back. He stood up very carefully and away they went.

"CHEEP, CHEEP, CHEEP!" exclaimed the Little Chicks.

"NEIGH!" said Horse with pleasure.

"OINK, OINK!" said the Ducks sadly.

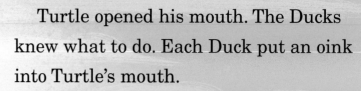

Turtle opened his mouth. The Ducks knew what to do. Each Duck put an oink into Turtle's mouth.

"OINK!" said Turtle, "OINK, OINK!"

Cow said, "QUACK!" She lay on the ground and opened her mouth. One by one, the Ducks took their quacks back from Cow.

"QUACK! QUACK! QUACK!" they called, as they plopped into the pond.

"MOO!" said the Hens. It was their turn to get their sound back. Each Hen gave Cow her moo.

"MOO-OO!" went Cow, happily, walking slowly to the far corner of the meadow, to chew grass in peace.

"CLUCK!" said Pig. "CLUCK, CLUCK!"

The Hens came to take their clucks from Pig.

"Well, Turtle," said Pig, "your job is almost done."

"OINK, OINK, OINK!" said Turtle, as loudly as he could. He opened his mouth and Pig took back his oink.

"OINK, OINK, OINK!" said Pig. "Thank you, Turtle, for being a good friend!"

Turtle beamed, and bobbed his head. What a wonderful day it had been!

Horse was neighing as he took the cheeping Little Chicks around the meadow.

Cow was mooing in the grass.

The Hens were clucking their way back to the barnyard.

Pig was oinking in a mud puddle.

The Ducks were quacking as they swam.

Yes, it had been a wonderful day, Turtle thought, and all because of the wind. But next time the wind rose and a storm blew through the farm, Turtle decided, he would open his mouth to try to catch a sound of his own.

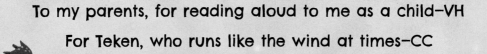

To my parents, for reading aloud to me as a child–VH
For Teken, who runs like the wind at times–CC

Library of Congress Cataloging-in-Publication data is on file with the publisher.

Text copyright © 2019 Virginia Howard
Illustrations copyright © 2019 Charlene Chua
First published in the United States of America in 2019 by Albert Whitman & Company
ISBN 978-0-8075-8735-5

Printed in China
10 9 8 7 6 5 4 3 2 1 WKT 22 21 20 19 18

Design by Aphee Messer and Anahid Hamparian

For more information about Albert Whitman & Company,
visit our website at www.albertwhitman.com

100 Years of Albert Whitman & Company
Celebrate with us in 2019!